This Ladybird Book belongs to:

_____

_____

_____

_____

Ladybird

This Ladybird retelling
by
Nicola Baxter

Published by Ladybird Books Ltd
80 Strand London WC2R 0RL
A Penguin Company
7 9 10 8

Printed in Italy

FAVOURITE TALES

The Big Pancake

illustrated
by
TONY KENYON

based on a traditional folk tale

Once upon a time there was a mother who had seven little boys – and they were *always* hungry!

One day seven hopeful little faces appeared around the kitchen door. "Mu-um," they said, "we're hungry!"

"You've just had your breakfast," laughed their mother. "What *am* I going to do with you? But, if you are *very* good little boys and *promise* to do the washing up, I'll make you the biggest pancake you've ever seen. And you can help."

So…

two hungry little boys cracked the
eggs and…

two hungry little boys measured
the milk and…

two hungry little boys weighed the flour and…

one hungry little boy mixed it all together (and got quite a lot on the floor!).

Then their mother heated some oil in a huge frying pan and poured in the mixture.

Soon delicious smells of cooking filled the kitchen and it was time to turn the pancake over.

"Toss it!" cried the seven hungry little boys, running for cover. "Please, Mum!"

So their mother tossed the pancake high into the air.

But while it was cooking, *the pancake* had been thinking.

"If I stay here, I will be gobbled right up by those seven hungry little boys. I must escape!"

And when the little boys' mother tossed the pancake into the air, it seized its chance.

With a *flip* and a *flop* the big pancake did a back somersault and landed on the kitchen floor! Then it rolled straight out of the door.

"Stop!" cried the seven hungry
little boys and their mother.
"We want to eat you!"

"Oh no," thought the big
pancake. And it rolled off down
the road.

Soon the pancake passed a man
in his garden.

"Stop!" cried the man. "I'd like to
eat you!" But the pancake just
rolled faster.

"I don't want to be eaten," it
said. "Seven hungry little boys
couldn't catch me. Their mother
couldn't catch me. And I won't let
you catch me!"

But the man put down his
spade and chased after the
big pancake.

Next the pancake passed a cat sitting on a wall.

"Stop!" miaowed the cat. "I'd like to eat you!" But the pancake just rolled faster.

"I don't want to be eaten," it said. "Seven hungry little boys couldn't catch me. Their mother couldn't catch me. A man couldn't catch me. And I won't let *you* catch me!"

But the cat jumped off the wall
and ran after the big pancake.

Further on the pancake passed a cockerel sitting on a gate.

"Stop!" crowed the cockerel. "I'd like to eat you!" But the pancake just rolled faster.

"I don't want to be eaten," it said. "Seven hungry little boys couldn't catch me. Their mother couldn't catch me. A man couldn't catch me. A cat couldn't catch me. And I won't let *you* catch me!"

But the cockerel jumped off the gate and flapped after the big pancake.

Round the corner the pancake passed a duck on a pond.

"Stop!" quacked the duck. "I'd like to eat you!" But the pancake just rolled faster.

"I don't want to be eaten," it said. "Seven hungry little boys couldn't catch me. Their mother couldn't catch me. A man couldn't catch me. A cat couldn't catch me. A cockerel couldn't catch me. And I won't let *you* catch me!"

But the duck paddled to the edge of the pond and waddled after the big pancake.

Before long the pancake passed a cow in a field.

"Stop!" mooed the cow. "I'd like to eat you!" But the pancake just rolled faster.

"I don't want to be eaten," it said. "Seven hungry little boys couldn't catch me. Their mother couldn't catch me. A man couldn't catch me. A cat couldn't catch me. A cockerel couldn't catch me. A duck couldn't catch me. And I won't let *you* catch me!"

But the cow pushed through the fence and galloped after the big pancake.

In some woodland, near a river, the pancake passed a pig.

"Where are you off to in such a hurry?" grunted the pig.

"I don't want to be eaten," said the pancake. "Seven hungry little boys couldn't catch me. Their mother couldn't catch me. A man couldn't catch me. A cat couldn't catch me. A cockerel couldn't catch me. A duck couldn't catch me. A cow couldn't catch me. And I won't let *you* catch me!"

"But I wouldn't dream of such a thing!" said the pig. "I'm on your side!"

"Well," said the pancake to the pig. "Could you help me to cross this river? Pancakes can't swim, you see."

"No problem," snorted the pig. "Just climb onto my nose and I will carry you across."

So the big pancake climbed onto the pig's nose. But the pig gave a chuckle and tossed the pancake high into the air.

Flip! Flop! This time there was no escape. The pancake fell right into the pig's open mouth and was gobbled up straightaway.

Just then the cow and the duck
and the cockerel and the cat
and the man and the mother
and the seven hungry little
boys came running up.

"Have you seen a big pancake?" they panted.

"Well," smiled the pig, "was it a *very* big pancake? Was it a lovely golden brown? Did it roll along on its side like a wheel?"

"*YES!*" they all yelled.

The pig licked his lips. "It was *DELICIOUS*!" he said.